Helicopters

Written by Kristen Beam

PIONEER VALLEY EDUCATIONAL PRESS, INC.

Here is a helicopter.

Helicopters can fly in the sky.

Helicopters can be big and they can be small.

The helicopter is going over the ocean.

The helicopter is going up, up, up.

Look at this helicopter.
It can help
put out a fire.

13

Look at this helicopter. The helicopter can help rescue people.

Helicopters

sky

helicopter

ocean

fire